Originally published in Denmark as
PRINSEN OG TIGGERDRENGEN by
Gutenberghus Gruppen, Copenhagen.

ISBN: 0-7172-8320-8

Disney's

THE PRINCE AND THE PAUPER

GROLIER
BOOKS

For many years England had a wise and good
King. The people were happy under his rule.
But by and by, the good King fell ill.

Soon the greedy captain of the guard,
Captain Pete, saw his chance to rob and
terrorize the people.

Without firewood to heat their
simple homes and enough food to
eat, people suffered terribly
throughout the land.

It seemed that no one could save the kingdom
from the thieving Captain Pete, until one day. . .

"Kindling! Fresh kindling!" called Mickey.
Beside him, Goofy shouted, "Get your snow-
cones here! Plain and rock and twig!" The two
friends were hungry and cold, too, but they tried
to make the best of things.

Suddenly, a coach full of Captain Pete's soldiers spun around a corner, spraying snow in Mickey's and Goofy's faces. Mickey's dog, Pluto, shook the snow from his snout and took off after them.

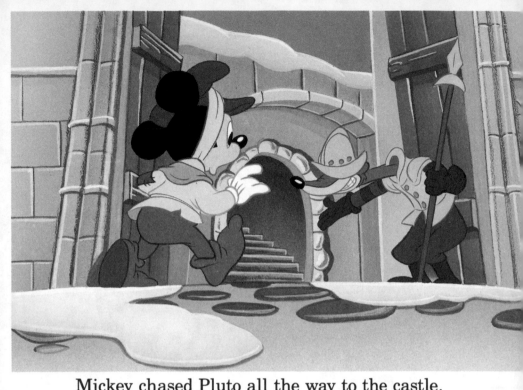

Mickey chased Pluto all the way to the castle. When one of Pete's guards caught sight of Mickey, he bowed so low that his nose almost touched the ground. "Welcome home, young Prince!" he said.

"You fool!" growled Captain Pete. "Don't you
know the Prince is still up in his room?" He
grabbed Mickey and was about to throw him out,
when the Prince called down to Captain Pete.
"That is no way to treat one of my subjects!
Unhand the lad and send him up to me."

As Mickey tried to find the Prince's room, he stared at the luxurious castle furnishings. He was so busy looking around that he forgot to watch where he was going. With a loud crash, he stumbled into several suits of armor.

Just then the Prince appeared. He was about
to greet Mickey when the helmets toppled onto
each of their heads!

Mickey and the Prince pulled off their helmets
and gasped.

"You look just like me!" cried Mickey.

"No, no, no!" cried the Prince. "You mean, you
look just like me. Exactly like me!"

Then the Prince had an idea. "I could take your
place for just one day. I'm tired of being a prince,"
he said. "I'm tired of studying and fencing and
never having time for myself. I'd like to see
what's going on outside these castle walls."

"If we swapped clothes,"
he told Mickey, "you
could live like a prince
for a while. And I could
walk around the kingdom —
just like an ordinary citizen!"

"But I don't know how to be a prince," said
Mickey.

"Don't worry!" said the Prince, as he gave
Mickey some royal clothes. "To govern, you need
only to say, 'Splendid idea. I'm glad I thought of
it.' and 'Guards, seize him!'"

The Prince put on Mickey's
clothes, climbed through the
window, and slid down a vine.
"I'll be back in the wink of
an eye," he called.

Mistaking the Prince for Mickey, Captain
Pete grabbed him as soon as he reached the
ground. Then he placed the Prince in a catapult
and fired him over the castle wall!

"And stay out!" Captain Pete shouted.

The Prince landed on his face in the snow, and Goofy and Pluto ran over to help him up. As soon as Pluto sniffed the Prince, he knew it wasn't his master, Mickey. So Pluto trotted off to the castle gate to wait for the real Mickey.

"Gawrsh, Mickey!" cried Goofy. "You shouldn't jump over walls and land on your head like that. You could get hurt!"

Of course, the Prince had no idea who Goofy was.

"I'm Goofy, remember?" said Mickey's friend.

"So I see, my good man," the Prince mumbled. "But I really must be going. Ta ta."

Now Goofy was really confused. Mickey had certainly never talked this way before!

Once the Prince
managed to get away
from Goofy, he began to enjoy his new
surroundings.

"What a nice little place," he said to
himself. "I really must try to come
here more often."

The Prince was enjoying his walk when he spotted a little dog. Because he'd never had a pet before, he thought it would be fun to play with the little fellow. But the little dog had bigger friends, who thought chasing the Prince was even more fun!

Back at the castle, Mickey was quickly becom-
ing bored with the life of a prince. He didn't like
spending his day taking all those lessons — not
when he could be eating instead!

Mickey licked his lips as Donald, the Prince's butler, carved a giant turkey. Mickey was about to help himself, but Donald pushed him away.

"Uh, uh, uh, Your Highness," said Donald. "Not yet! Remember, I have to taste it first. What if one of your enemies is trying to poison you?"

"What enemies?" asked Mickey. But Donald didn't answer. His mouth was too full. And before Mickey could get a taste, Donald gobbled up everything on the platter!

Outside the castle,
the real Prince quickly
discovered that the greatest
enemies of the townspeople
were the King's own soldiers!

Captain Pete had been ordering his men to steal everything they could carry! The Prince was horrified.

"As your Prince, I command you to give back everything that you have stolen!" he declared.

"Prince?" scoffed a soldier. "Oh, I get it. You forgot to wear your crown today," he said as he clobbered the Prince with a pumpkin. "How's that for a crown?"

Then the Prince remembered something. "I can prove I'm the Prince!" he shouted. He showed them his Royal Ring, the only thing he had brought from the castle.

Everyone bowed before the Prince when they saw it — even the soldier who had a cart of stolen food. "It *is* the Prince!" he cried.

The Prince quickly took charge of the food and
began to give it back to the hungry people. He
handed out loaves of bread, and chickens, sausages
and hams, until all the food had been returned.

"Hooray for the Prince!" shouted the happy crowd.

Not everybody was happy about the Prince's kindness — least of all Captain Pete's spies, who ran off to tell him about what the Prince was up to. Pete quickly found the Prince and had him thrown into the castle dungeon!

Donald was imprisoned, too.

The Prince wept as he sat on the cold stone
floor. Because he had changed places with Mickey,
he had not been with his father when the King
died. And now Mickey, the pauper, would be
crowned King!

Suddenly there was the sound of heavy foot-
steps. Donald and the Prince peered through the
cell door to see a tall dark figure coming toward
them. He was carrying a very sharp axe.

"It's the royal executioner!" gasped Donald.
"Captain Pete must have sent him!"

The Prince and Donald shuddered as the
executioner approached. To their great surprise,
he tripped on his long robe and knocked the
guards unconscious with the side of his axe.

"Gawrsh, I sure am sorry!" cried Goofy, as he
pulled off his hood. Donald grabbed the keys from
Goofy and unlocked the door.

Meanwhile, Captain Pete continued his evil plan. He was forcing Mickey to become the new king. To make sure that Mickey would obey his orders, Pete had kidnapped Pluto. Pete knew that Mickey would never do anything to put his dog in danger. With Mickey on the throne, Captain Pete would control the kingdom!

Just as the crown was about to be placed on
Mickey's head, Mickey ducked and said, "Stop!
Captain Pete is a traitor! Guards, seize him!"

"The boy is an imposter!" shouted Pete.

"But I am not!" called out the Prince, bursting
into the room. As he rushed toward Captain Pete,
he snatched a sword from a guard, and the fight
was on!

Goofy and Donald were doing their best to help
the Prince. Donald swung his axe and sliced the
ropes that held up the chandelier. It fell down on
a whole crowd of soldiers.

When the brave Prince knocked Pete's sword out of his hand, the townspeople cheered.

"Off to the dungeon with them!" commanded the Prince.

The townspeople tied up Pete and his men and led them away.

Then it was time for the ceremony. The real
Prince was crowned King, and the people could
feel safe once more with a kind and generous
ruler. The people all lived happily ever
after — thanks to Mickey, Goofy and Donald!